To renew or order library books visit
www.lincolnshire.gov.uk
You will require a Personal Identification Number.
Ask any member of staff for this

MORONEY.   152.41
When I'm Feeling Loved
£4.99

L5/9

The Five Mile Press

When I'm feeling loved
I feel like I could grow wings
and fly high up in the sky
amongst the stars.

To my special friend Debra – and in loving memory of her mum, Anita.

The Five Mile Press Pty Ltd
950 Stud Road Rowville
Victoria 3178 Australia
Email: publishing@fivemile.com.au
Website: www.fivemile.com.au

First published 2007

National Library of Australia Cataloguing-in-Publication data
Moroney, Trace
When I'm feeling loved.

For children
ISBN 978 1 74178 356 8 (hardback)
ISBN 978 1 74178 357 5 (paperback)

1. Love - Juvenile fiction. I. Title.

A823.3

Printed in China 5 4 3 2 1

Prints of artwork produced for this title are available for purchase.
Please email Trace Moroney on tracemoroney@xtra.co.nz for more information.

Background Notes for Parents

Self-esteem is the key

The greatest gift you can give your child is healthy self-esteem. Children who *feel valuable*, and who *trust themselves* have positive self-esteem. You can help your child *feel valuable* by spending quality time with him or her, playing games, reading books, or just listening. You can also help children *feel valuable* by helping them discover and become the person they want to be. Success follows people who genuinely *like who they are*.

However, happiness is more than just being successful. Helping your child gain the *self-trust* needed to deal with failure, loss, shame, difficulty and defeat is as important – if not more so – than succeeding or being best. When children trust themselves to handle painful feelings – fear, anger and sadness – they gain an *inner* security that allows them to embrace the world in which they live.

Each of these *FEELINGS* books has been carefully designed to help children better understand their feelings, and in doing so, gain greater autonomy (freedom) over their lives. Talking about feelings teaches children that it is normal to feel sad, or angry, or scared at times. With greater tolerance of painful feelings, children become free to enjoy their world, to feel secure in their abilities, and to be happy.

Feeling LOVED

Feeling loved brings a special sense of belonging, warmth and security to a child. Sometimes parents mistakenly believe that love is expressed through gifts and special treats, particularly when their child behaves well. However, most of the time, all your child will want is for you to spend time with them. Giving your child a hug or a smile, or being calm and patient especially in difficult situations are all everyday signs of love. In a busy life, giving your child the time and attention they need can be difficult. Yet the results are worth it. When your child experiences themselves as loved, they build a healthy self-esteem, and become free to love others and engage the world with less fear.

Written by a Melbourne child psychologist

When I'm feeling loved
I feel warm and safe and protected . . .
like being wrapped up in clouds
of cotton wool.

Feeling loved makes me feel

Some things that make me
feel loved are . . .
when a friend puts
their arm around me
and says "Thank you
for being a good friend" . . .

or, when my dog Poppy
licks my face . . .

or, when Mum or Dad tucks me
into bed at night and says,
"I love you my little snuggle-bunny."

Feeling loved makes me feel strong . . .
so when something difficult happens
I feel more confident to try to work it out by myself.

When I'm feeling loved
I feel more happy and more confident
with the person that I am.

Being loved teaches me how
to love others . . . and myself.

Love is so easy to share!

I LOVE being loved!
Do you?